READY, SET, MISSION!

Adapted by Nate Cosby

Based on the screenplay by The Wibberleys and Ted Elliott & Terry Rossio and Tim Firth

Based on a story by Hoyt Yeatman

Executive Producers Mike Stenson, Chad Oman, Duncan Henderson, David James

Produced by Jerry Bruckheimer

Directed by Hoyt Yeatman

Copyright © 2009 Disney Enterprises, Inc.

JERRY BRUCKHEIMER FILMS™ and JERRY BRUCKHEIMER FILMS TREE LOGO™
are all trademarks. All rights reserved. Unauthorized use is prohibited.

Printed in the United States of America

First edition

1 3 5 7 9 10 8 6 4 2

Library of Congress Catalog Card Number on file

ISBN 978-1-4231-1943-2

Disney PRESS

NEW YORK

Hi. I'm Darwin.

Juarez, Blaster, Speckles, Mooch, and I are a specially trained group of secret agents. Together, we are the G-Force.

Ben, our boss, gave us our mission: to get into Leonard Saber's house, copy a computer file, and get out again—without being caught. Saber is a rich businessman. But we suspected he had created something dangerous.

The night we put our plan into action, Saber was throwing a party.
We dove right into his courtyard.

Speckles, the mole, was responsible for guiding the rest of us through Saber's house. He was positioned underground with his computers. He watched the entire mission through Mooch the fly's tiny camera and used radio equipment to tell us what to do.

Since I'm the team leader, I led the way. I entered Saber's mansion by disguising myself as part of a woman's fur coat.

Getting inside the house was easy. Next I had to find Saber's office upstairs and copy the file.

I found the office, but it was under guard!
Mooch knew what to do—he buzzed
around the guard's head to annoy him.

The guard was distracted just long
enough for me to sneak by without being
seen.

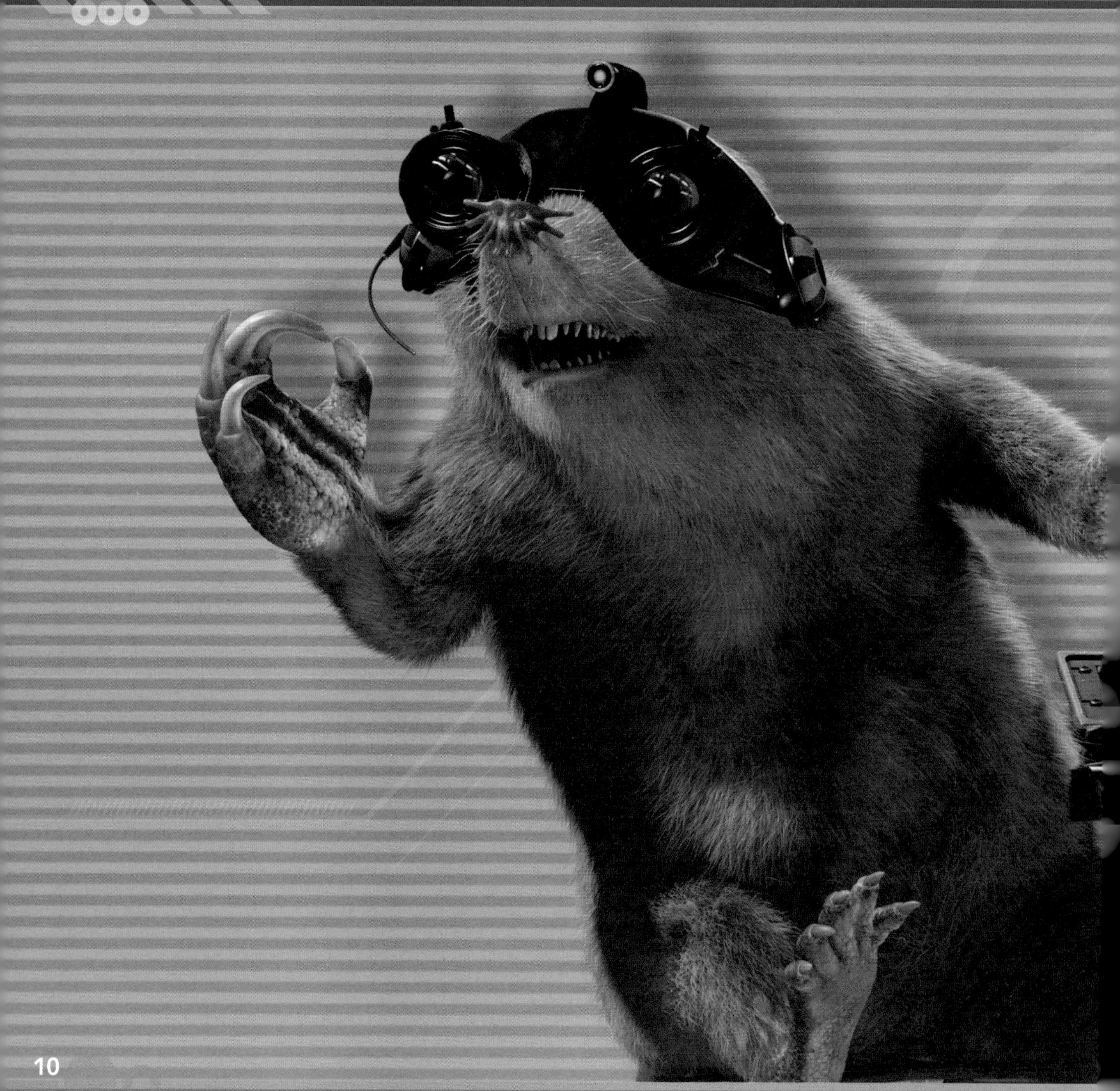

I found it! But just then, Speckles warned me that Saber was on his way up to the office. I was running out of time. To stall Saber, Mooch flew right up into his nose!

PING! I finished copying the file and ran to my escape route—the office fireplace.

Juarez and Blaster were stationed on the roof, and they had lowered a rope down the chimney so I could climb to safety. But Saber clapped his hands—and the fireplace roared to life! I grabbed the rope and Juarez and Blaster pulled me up.

The fire was right on my tail—and it was *hot*! The flames singed my fur a little, but I made it to the roof.

Juarez and Blaster were ready to leave when we saw something terrible: a guard dog had found Speckles's hole and was trying to eat him!

Blaster sprang into action! He leaped off the roof and opened his parasail. Gliding down, he bonked the top of the guard dog's head—then he got stuck on a bush!

Juarez and I jumped off the roof, too. Juarez stopped the dog by tying up its mouth, and then she got Blaster down from the bush.

Once we'd regrouped and taken care of the dog, we took off our spy equipment and made a run for the exit gate. We were home free!

ACME

ACME EXTERMINATORS

CALL US ANYTIME DAY OR NIG

1-

8

As we neared the gate, an exterminator pulled up in his truck. A masked man climbed out of the truck and sprayed us with something that made us fall to the ground, coughing.

A crowd of people from the party had gathered to see what was going on. The exterminator scooped up all of us and told the people not to worry. He'd taken care of the pest problem. He threw us into the truck, got behind the wheel, and pulled away. As the truck drove off, the exterminator took off his mask....

It was our boss, Ben! He'd disguised himself as an exterminator, and we'd pretended to play dead so he could take us away.

We'd made it out of Saber's house with the file! Mission accomplished!